MW01225185

Colossal Fossil

The Dinosaur Riddle Book

by Mike Thaler

America's Riddle King

illustrated by Rick Brown

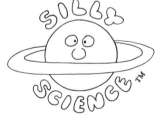

SILLY SCIENCE™

Scientific American BOOKS FOR YOUNG READERS

W. H. Freeman and Company • New York

For Marc Gave,
whose patience saved him from
being a patient

Text copyright © 1994 by Mike Thaler.
Illustrations copyright © 1994 by Rick Brown.
SILLY SCIENCE and logo are trademarks of Mike Thaler.
All rights reserved.

Printed on recycled paper in the United States of America.

Scientific American Books for Young Readers is an imprint of
W. H. Freeman and Company,
41 Madison Avenue, New York, NY 10010.

Library of Congress Cataloging-in-Publication Data
Thaler, Mike, 1936-
Colossal fossil / Mike Thaler.
ISBN 0-7167-6561-6. — ISBN 0-7167-6571-3 (pbk.)
1. Riddles, Juvenile. 2. Dinosaurs—Juvenile humor.
[1. Dinosaurs—Wit and humor. 2. Riddles. 3. Jokes.]
I. Brown, Rick, 1946- ill. II. Title.
PN6371.5.T47 1994 818'.5402—dc20 94-16084 CIP AC

10 9 8 7 6 5 4 3 2 1

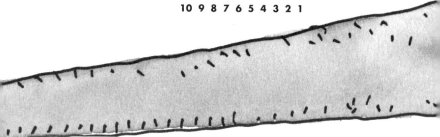

Knock, knock. Who's there?
Jurassic. Jurassic who?

Jur-as-sic as I am if these riddles make you laugh.

What dinosaurs directed traffic?

Tricera-cops.

What happened when "terrible lizards" had head-on collisions?

There were Tyrannosaurus wrecks.

What do you get if you cross a pig with a dinosaur?

Knock, knock. Who's there?
Dinosaur. Dinosaur who?

Dinosaur a great movie last night.

What dinosaur was into hip-hop?

O.V. Rap-tor.

What dinosaur was made of plastic blocks?

Lego-saurus.

Sega-saurus.

What dinosaur played video games?

What did the saber-toothed tiger say when it got stuck in tar?

This is the pits!

Why did the saber-toothed tiger lose the Indy 500?

He made a pit stop.

What dinosaur bossed everyone around?

Tyrant-osaurus.

Where did young dinosaurs spend their summers?

At Camp-to-saurus.

Why were pterosaurs always in debt?

Because they had big bills.

What flying reptile could go anywhere?

All-terrain-odon.

What prehistoric creature had a hole in the middle?

A donut-saur.

What prehistoric beast could add, subtract, and multiply?

What was the dinosaurs' favorite movie?

The Lizard of Oz.

What dinosaur wrote romantic novels?

Emily Brontë-saurus.

What dinosaur could you ride at a rodeo?

Bronco-saurus.

What dinosaur lived in New York City?

Bronx-osaurus.

What dinosaur lived in Canada?

What dinosaur lived in the desert?

Sahara-tops.

What dinosaur was a great boxer?

Muhammad Ali-saurus.

What do you give a constipated Tyrannosaurus?

Rex-Lax.

What dinosaur hurt its leg?

Ankle-saur.

What dinosaur graduated from medical school?

Diploma-docus.

What dinosaur knew about fine wine?

Connois-saur.

What dinosaur ran a beauty parlor?

Hair-dressaur.

What dinosaurs were the friendliest?

What dinosaur could you mail in for NBA stickers?

Tri-cereal-tops.

What was the prehistoric creatures' favorite TV show?

The Dinah Shore Show.

During what period did most dinosaurs date?

The Flirtatious Period.

During what era didn't dinosaurs clean up?

The Mess-ozoic Era.

What do you call a prehistoric Girl Scout?

Brownie-saurus.

During what period did dinosaurs have music?

Third period—right after gym.

What prehistoric creature was a popular singer?

Madonna-saur.

What dinosaur knew a lot of synonyms?

Thesaurus.

Dinosaur Owner's Manual

Get a big litter box.

Get a long leash.

Don't let it sleep at the foot of your bed.

Don't feed it from the dinner table.

What sounds did sleeping prehistoric creatures make?

Dino-snores.

Where did prehistoric creatures go shopping?

At a dime-a-store.

What do you get if you cut a Dimetrodon in half?

Do you have change for a Dime-etrodon?

Two Nickel-etrodons.

What teenage dinosaurs went to private schools?

What two kinds of dinosaurs took pictures?

Camera-saurus and Photo-ceratops.

What dinosaurs were the best story tellers?

The ones with the longest tales.

On what dinosaur could you hang your neckwear?

Tie-rack-osaurus.

What dinosaur wore lots of gold chains and was in *Rocky 3*?

Mr. T. Rex.

What do you call a reptile snowstorm?

A lizard blizzard.

What was a Tyrannosaurus's favorite kind of food?

Tex-Rex.

They wore one watch on a front leg and one on a back leg because they lived in two time zones.

They each had their own ZIP code.

When they stepped on a scale, it read, "To be continued..."

What do you call a prehistoric creature with a big pimple?

An Icky-sore.

**Knock, knock. Who's there?
Saber tooth. Saber tooth who?**

Saber tooth for the Tooth Fairy.

What dinosaur wouldn't you ask to wash your dishes?

A Break-iosaurus.
However, you could ask a Stegosaurus,
because it had lots of plates.

What dinosaurs were the noisiest?

Triceratops...they all had horns.

What did the mother dinosaur do on Christmas Eve?

She raptor children's presents.

Why did the little dinosaurs go to the beach on Christmas Eve?

So they could come back with Sandy Claws.

What newspaper did dinosaurs publish?

The Fossil Record.

How do scientists know dinosaurs rode on trains?

They found their tracks.

How do scientists know dinosaurs liked music?

Because they found their old rock records.

Why did dinosaurs get so tired?

Because they walked the earth for millions of years.

What do you call a huge dinosaur skeleton?

A colossal fossil.